Wobble Bear

IAN WHYBROW AND CAROLINE JAYNE CHURCH

OXFORD
UNIVERSITY PRESS

THIS is the way
that some bears crawl.

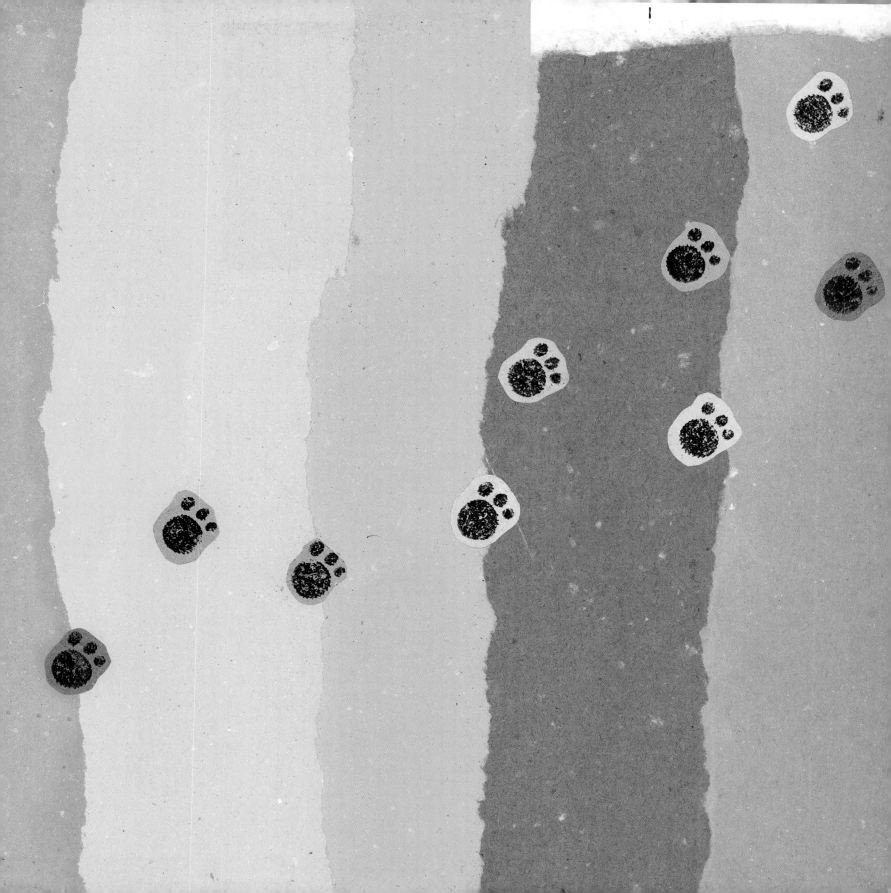

OXFORD

UNIVERSITY PRESS

Great Clarendon Street, Oxford OX2 6DP

Oxford University Press is a department of the University of Oxford.
It furthers the University's objective of excellence in research, scholarship,
and education by publishing worldwide in

Oxford New York

Auckland Bangkok Buenos Aires Cape Town Chennai
Dar es Salaam Delhi Hong Kong Istanbul Karachi Kolkata
Kuala Lumpur Madrid Melbourne Mexico City Mumbai Nairobi
São Paulo Shanghai Taipei Tokyo Toronto

Oxford is a registered trade mark of Oxford University Press
in the UK and in certain other countries

British Library Cataloguing in Publication Data available

ISBN 0-19-279126-5 Hardback
ISBN 0-19-272563-7 Paperback

1 3 5 7 9 10 8 6 4 2

Printed in Singapore

What about Wobble Bear?

Wobble Bear has learned to walk,

so everywhere he goes,

he likes to wibble-wobble

on his wibbly wobbly toes.

Early in the morning, he goes to Mummy's room, tries Mummy's shoes on -

boom,
boom,
boom!

'Far too early,' Mum yawns.

'Go back to bed!'

Wobble Bear walks
on his daddy instead.

'What a quick eater!
Where's that breakfast gone?'
Wobble's in a hurry now to turn the music on.

Look at Wobble dancing, round and round and round. Now he's feeling dizzy -

-whoops!-

- all fall down!

Down you come,
Wobble Bear.
Walk, don't dash!

Now he's found a puddle so it's

splash,

splash,

splash!

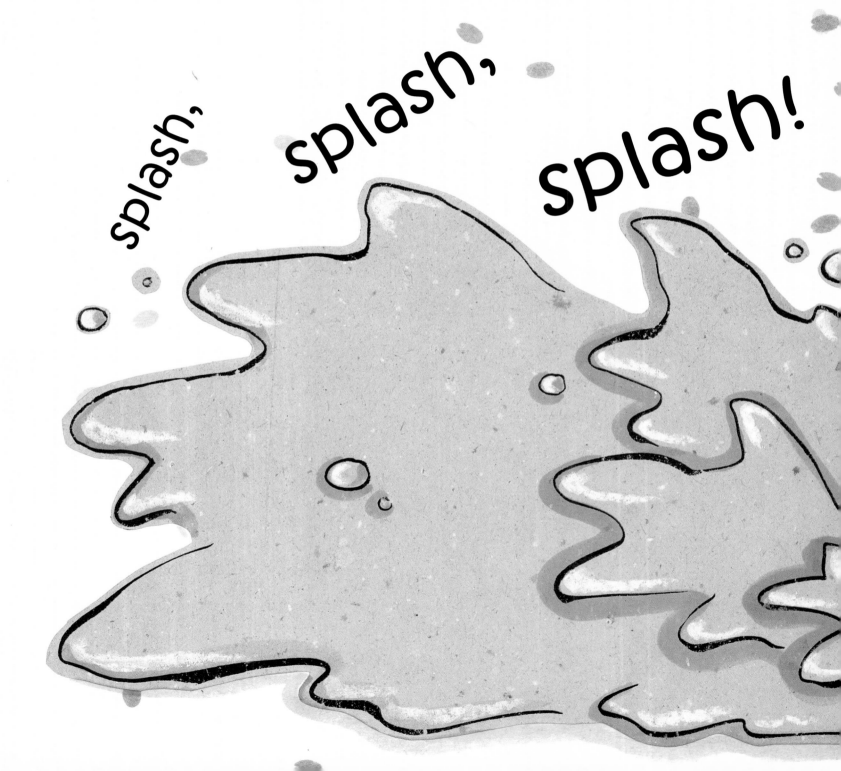

Home through the park now, time to go back.
Wobble does his duck-walk.
Quack-quack-quack!

Wobble Bear walks
where the other
bears ride.

First he walks the see-saw, then he walks the slide.

Walk,

walk,

walk,

walk!

Wobble's never still . . .

. . . till it's
time to
take a walk
up the
wooden
hill.

Wobble squeaked
a whisper.
This is what
he said.

'Can't walk. Too tired.
Carry me up to bed.'

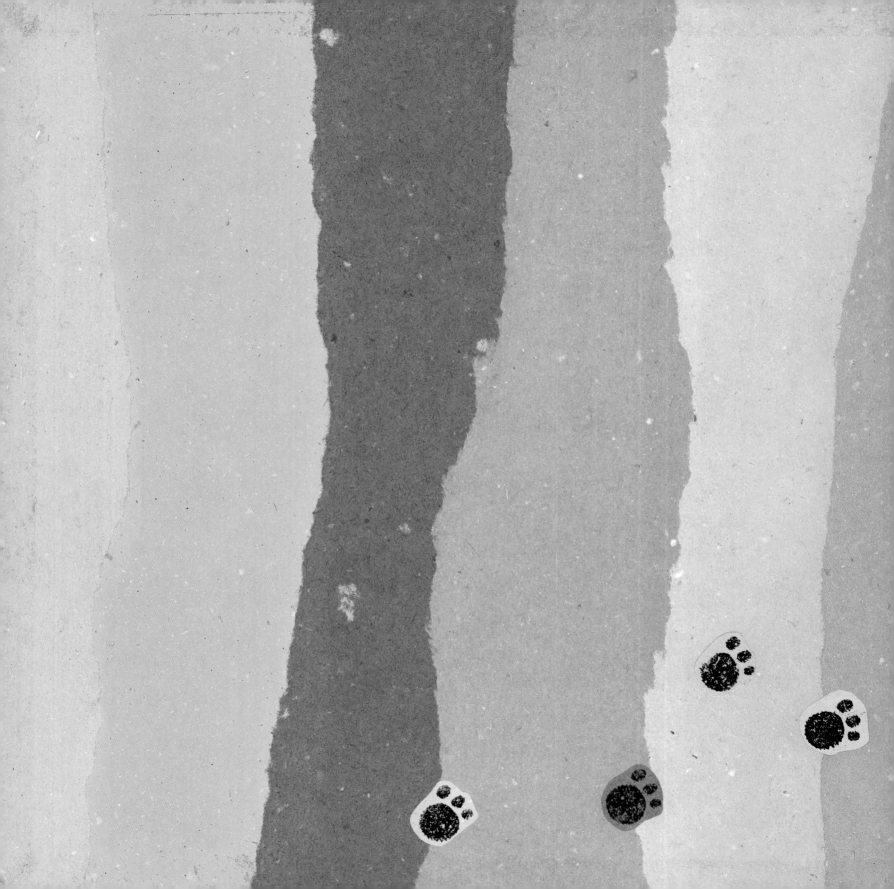